SCALING NEW HEIGHTS
Poems and Prose

PAKARAIMA WRITERS

www.middleroadpublishers.ca

Making Literature See The Light Of Day

Library and Archives Canada Cataloguing in Publication

ISBN (paper) 978-1-990765-02-5

Editor: Ken Puddicombe

Cover photograph courtesy

VivechughFreeImages.com

Cover Design by Ken Puddicombe

CREDITS

- Ian McDONALD
    - *Going Away* published in *The Garden* 2021 by MiddleRoad Publishers
    - *The Petal Shivers* published in *The Garden* 2021 by MiddleRoad Publishers
    - *Throwing a Hummingbird* published in *The Garden* 2021 by MiddleRoad Publishers
- Janet NAIDU
    - *The Unknown Path* Published 2005 in *Rainwater* copyright Janet Naidu
    - *Trails of Treasures* Published in Winged Heart 1999 Greenheart Press
- Ken PUDDICOMBE
    - *I Am Who I Am* published in *Unfathomable And Other Poems* 2020 by MiddleRoad Publishers
    - *Best Before* published in *Down Independence Boulevard And Other Stories* 2017 by MiddleRoad Publishers
    - *A Lovers Tryst* published in *Down Independence Boulevard And Other Stories* 2017 by MiddleRoad Publishers
- James C. RICHMOND
    - *Guyana's Seawall* Published in *On the Window of My Skin* 2006 copyright James Richmond
    - *Like Amazon Rain I Dance* Published in *On the Window of My Skin* 2006 copyright James Richmond
    - *Where Pomeroon Meets* Published 1997 *Where Pomeroon Meets* copyright James Richmond

"I tell you

this is no magnificent province

no El Dorado for me

no streets paved with gold

but a bruising and battering for self-preservation..."

—Martin Carter (1927-1997)—

Dedicated

To all writers who seek an outlet for their vivid imagination, wake up one morning and see their work in print and experience the marvel of it all!

FOREWORD

To begin with, I am thankful to the founder and past President from 2005 to 2017, Janet Naidu, poet and writer, for her dedication to the arts, in creating a space for poets and writers to come together; for her more than three decades as a community leader and in fostering diversity and inclusion. The Pakaraima Writers Association has fostered many literary luncheon celebrations, where poetry, stories and authors' published works have served the community in Toronto through readings.

Serving as President from 2018, as a poet and writer and community leader, I take great pleasure in continuing this important space in our community, where many of our writers have been inspired to write and to be published, as well as to be supported and share their works at our events.

Ever since the pandemic, Pakaraima Writers Association has convened poetry medleys online and has successfully brought together poets and writers of Guyanese and Caribbean backgrounds in the diaspora, including Canada, Guyana, Barbados, Trinidad and the USA. to share their many writings, be they expressions of love, fear, unity, cultural heritage, social consciousness, isolation and inspiration.

I extend appreciation to Mr. Ken Puddicombe, an established writer and publisher of MiddleRoad Publishers, and a member of the Pakaraima Writers Association, who made a refreshing suggestion for Pakaraima to consider the creation of this Anthology, immediately following our recent readings on a virtual platform. After many years of in-person readings and since the virtual readings, this was an innovative and welcomed idea for the poets and writers to submit their works—poetry and short stories.

Deepest thanks to all of the contributors to this Pakaraima Anthology.

Habeeb Alli
President, Pakaraima Writers and Artists Association

Table of Contents

HERITAGE

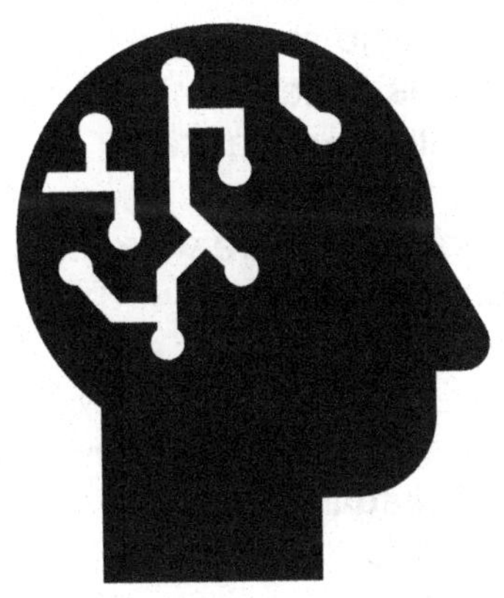

1. I ONCE MET A GIRL
by Habeeb ALLI

I once met a girl
Standing on the moon
The stars bowed to her
It was a meeting beyond the blue

She laughed giddily at my jokes.
Born in Canje she made sure
she carried her mother's culture
Inside her heart like a red dress
on a summer's day!

This is far from the truth and reality
of her trueness of who she really
is beyond the pages of academia.
But her warmth will make Kaieteur
look like a teapot on the fire.
The generosity, love and care will melt
a hard-heart coolie
worse than green heart

Luck is the fortune of the unprepared
On the hilltops of Niagara
Cascades my dreams
Into her starry eyes
like Purple Rain all again!

Will the Sheherazade of
Pakaraima rise again?

2. GUYTRACKS BROOKLYN
by Jerome BRANCHE

(for Cyril and Cecil)

the romans knew
and nodded
was earth was come
for earth

they'd heard it in the trees
like wind wresting
leaves
some brown some green
some in between
some sudden

all fallen
earth seeking earth

wasn't kite season
the scratching at the sky
of spirits triumphant
wings wide let's fly?

wasn't Christmas chorus
Christ came for us
rumcake and raisins
like child eyes blazin'?

wasn't August Monday
run around funday?

was wake house and wailing
was stout hearts failing
coffee biscuits and black shirts
a stifling of mirth

was quickening earth

the romans felt it.

3. MY LIFE
by Alicia DANIELS

(A Personal Reflection)

My life is a journey that has not yet ended,
A picture not yet fully developed.

From the day I was born,
I was destined to be a wonder to many.
I have seen many good starts and many failed efforts,
But I have also seen many greater, determined attempts made.

I have had leaps and bounds, ups and downs.
My failures, successes, joy and sadness
Are tools of wisdom and strength.

I have not learnt everything nor likely to,
So I'm thankful for a heavenly father,
Who knows the weight I can bear,
Unto Him I can cast all my cares.

Although I may not be an Einstein,
David, Napoleon nor Daniel,
My impact is still as uniquely earthshaking.

My life is not my own, I've come to realize,

But the One who sits on His throne on
high.

As my life is sustained,
Greater is yet to come.
So don't judge me wrongfully, based on
where you think I'm from,
Conform me not to present trials.

For in a season, you'll see greater
progress,
Instead of frustrated tears.

I have tried to be like others and failed
at doing so.
I then understood, I can only be me.

The path I now travel is narrow and
even lonely at times,
But whatever point I'm at,
My heavenly father is there to bear me
up and make me shine.

4. THE BALLAD OF CHRISTOPHER STEVENSON

By Francis Quamina FARRIER

Christopher Stephenson from Tiger Bay,
Was one of the bravest almost every day.
He had a dray cart that rode the street,
A job he did for whoever he would meet.

He worked that dray cart to earn some cash,
But his hard-working horse he never did lash.
He'd pack that cart with lots of load,
And deliver the goods to intended goal.

Christopher Stephenson had a lovely wife,
And four smart kids that shared his life.
He worked liked a dog and sweat like a horse,
For his wretched life he had no remorse.

Then one day he left his home,
With his horse and cart but not to roam.
He headed down south to Sussex Street,
Now that was the day his destiny he'd meet.

Gidde-up, gidde-up and the horse did run,
For Christopher Stephenson that was fun.
From Avenue of the Republic, down High Street,
clippy-a-tee, clippy-a-tee, the horse's feet.

Then into Saffon Street the cart did go,
But Christopher Stephenson did not know,
That death was awaiting, so near for him,

So a soft song of joy he started to sing.

Gidde-up, gidde-up to the horse he sang.
Christopher Stephenson was a happy man.
His wife was away in New Amsterdam,
Their children he cared like a responsible man.

Fixing their meals and being a good dad.
Something that's not such a popular fad.
A man is a man when he cares for his kids.
As Christopher Stephenson did all their bids.

He did many things that were oh, so good.
And cared for his children as a father should.
His horse, too, he loved with all his heart,
And made sure it had a well-working cart.

Gidde-up, gidde-up, they raced that day.
Into Sussex Street, for that was the way.
To the scene of two unfortunate men.
Down in a manhole, a poisonous pen.

A crowd had gathered to view the scene.
Every Tom, Dick, Harrylall and inquisitive Jean.
They wanted to know what was going on.
Always inquisitive since they were born.

Christopher Stephenson also wanted to know,
Was it an accident or just a show.
So many standing and looking down.
To two unfortunate men deep underground.

He stopped his cart and tied his horse.
And marched through the crowd, he was the first,

To climb right down into the poisonous hole.
No one knew what was his heroic goal.

The two men were there as though asleep.
The poisonous gas reduced them so deep.
Christopher Stephenson took a very quick look,
Then did something brave one only reads in a book.

He scooped up the first man, and started to climb,
To save that first victim, it was so sublime.
Up, out of the manhole Christopher went.
He was an angel who the Lord had sent.

Up on the street he laid him down,
A stranger in distress who he had found.
Then back in the manhole he did return.
It was his last day on earth since he was born.

"Here he comes with the second man."
Cried an onlooker whose name was Dan.
But Christopher Stephenson was getting weak.
The fresh air above he wanted to seek.

Yes, Christopher Stephenson was now so weak,
It was obvious that he could hardly speak.
So slowly to the ground he did descend,
His life here on earth was about to end.

The poisonous gas he did inhale.
More than was good for a strong young male.
So down on the ground he laid himself out,
He was a dying man it was no doubt.

Out at the corner of the crowd was his horse.
Looking at that animal one saw much remorse.

Thinking that his master, he had taken there,
And now in his death, he had shown no fear.

The poisonous gas had filled his lungs,
And swirling around like vicious hounds.
They attacked his brain, it was no lie,
That Christopher Stephenson was about to die.

He laid him down and closed his eyes,
And asked for forgiveness for any lies.
Yes, he laid him down and his soul passed away,
From that great Hero of Tiger Bay.

And up in heaven all the angels sang,
A welcome chorus for the dray-cart man,
As through the clouds his soul wended its way.
Here comes The Hero of Tiger Bay.

5. TAPESTRY
by Lisa FREEMANTLE

Feb 11, 2021

History stretches forward in time,
touches us on the shoulder
and seeps into our skin

We are build-ed chronicles, molded sagas;
preordained re-occurring themes,
rooted from deep within

Though our life journeys are individual,
they are in themselves not unique
Recessed thoughts percolate;
their effects indirect, oblique

For we are a tapestry of long agos,
here and nows and tomorrows;
woven threads of past joys,
present stresses and future sorrows

Who we were, who we are
and who we will be
are all one in the same, actually
They are transected yet connected,
infected with one another;
we are inexorably linked
to our inner father, mother, sister, brother

The bonds are inescapable,
no matter where we turn,
they pull and push

and these entwining strands yearn
to fabricate, cultivate
and create a new telling
of our joined story:
past history, future memory compelling
It is an eternally winding
and meandering life tale
fed fresh by our present-day minutia and detail

So…ensure your knitted fibres remain
moral, just and strong

for it is to future generations
that they will evermore belong

6. SEPARATION
by Peter JAILALL

On arrival in the far away country
I worked hard
In the open cane fields
For the white sahibs
Who were strict, loud and brutal.
I endured their lashes
And curses.
Punishment and poverty
Were my lot

More than one hundred and eighty years
have passed.
Life is still hard
And the pay is not so great.
I live in a little red house.
I live on the bank
Of a big river facing the mighty Atlantic.
Yellow mangoes hang
In the golden sun
And monkeys banter in the tree tops

I grow rice
I plant bindi and bhaji
Moulding their roots with cow dung.
I rear cattle and feed my fowls
And I'm settled with my large extended
In my new country Guyana

I promise I will visit you someday

Search for you
And the little village
I left behind

I think of you often
And wonder what my life would have been
If the *Harkat* didn't come to my door
On that rainy day.

7. THE PETAL SHIVERS
by Ian McDONALD

come with me my love share this perfection
morning dew has vanished from the grass
one translucent drop remains on a single
petal
shining dot reflects the sun's fast rising glory
soon it will be gone such wonders do not last
there a sudden wind shivers the red petal
the moment's gleam of beauty gone I am
content
there has been so much my love petals in the
wind

8. THE UNKNOWN PATH
by Janet NAIDU

In memory my brother Arnold Moonsammy Naidu whose whereabouts have remained unknown since 1972 in Columbia.

The endless years of a curious path
through jungles and borders,
with grated walls of another land
and its myriad ways,
very much confusing, chaining you down.
Coconut boats hurriedly fill
the sound of thunder in a dark forest.
Heavy boots of paramilitaries
near a guarded gate
keep us from the impossible search,
while pressing us against the wired fences
of our only chance for a hopeful horizon.

I grip your hand near me
moving through tunnels of darkness,
out of the chains that held you captive
inside maddening walls.

The reason for leaving home: dictatorship
and visions of betterment anywhere—
Even other young men who hardly knew
the corners of their villages,
who barely understood dark roads
across distant lands,
but who always watched the sun rising in the rhythm

of their fathers cutting cane,
found a way out in nightly escape.

I long for this miracle.
How will I know that path?

I once dreamed I saw you—
regrets and longing in your eyes
to be rescued—
and then I saw layers of the rainforest.

Have the decades of unknown whereabouts
lengthened far too long?
Who will find your footprints?

How do I know the location of your name?

9. FAATY-LEVEN by Petamber PERSAUD

only a lil chile
knows de real meaning of
faaty-leven

is sohmuch times
big people doz
ring e eaz
pull e hair
kanze e hed
an shout pon e

only a lil chile knows
wat is faaty-leven blows
foh being
faaty-leven times unwilling
faaty-leven times haadeaz

faaty-leven times
a chile
widout rights!

10. A LOVERS' TRYST
by Ken PUDDICOMBE

I was on my way to the Airport to catch my plane, passing through Kitty, a suburb at the east end of Georgetown when my cousin, Rex, pulled over to the side of the road. The entire trip had been like that: one long journey punctuated by frequent stops to refill a leaky radiator.

Rex pulled out the now familiar yellow plastic pail from the trunk and set off to fill it with water, but when I saw him duck into the Offtrack Betting Shop across the street I knew that it would be sometime before I saw him again.

I didn't mind the wait. I was in no hurry—there were another twelve hours before the flight and my body-clock had long since adjusted to the easy rhythm of the lifestyle in Guyana. I looked around and couldn't help thinking that while I would be back in Toronto the next day, life in Guyana would go on as usual, the same as it had over the last two decades while I was away. The fat pig: his enormous pink bulk taking over half the width of the trench across from me would still be siphoning his way through the muck; the women standing on the parapet gossiping would find something else to talk about; the men sitting around the table on the shop-bridge playing dominoes would be back to finish the bottle of rum or start another.

Suddenly, I noticed people running up the street, past the car. It was as if they had just received a news flash that looters were emptying stores in the shopping area, and they wanted part of the action. It alarmed me.

I turned to see where they were going. They were crowded around a woman outside a shack two house lots from where the car was stopped, and they all seemed to be caught up in the excitement as she repeatedly slammed a piece of lumber on the door of the shack. The piece of lumber was so large and unwieldy that she had to take hold of it several times to avoid it slipping from her grasp. But what really stood out was a red blotch at the back of her head: she was bleeding from a wound on the right side, the blood trickling down through her short, curly, black hair, settling on her shoulder. But she took no notice of it.

"Come out," the woman shouted as she hit the door repeatedly. "T'ink yuh can bust mah head and get away wid it, nuh?"

At last, after several bangs on the door, it gave way. A man emerged from the shack. She went up to him, pushed him with a sharp slap to his chest, and then, started to dance around him, sparring like a boxer in a prizefight. She kept him at bay while she took shots at his face. Meanwhile, the crowd milled around, laughing and clapping: the females encouraging the woman to stand up for her rights and the males teasing the man, asking whether he was a man or a mouse to *tekh all that beating from a woman*.

I thought the incident would work itself out and dismissed it. But a roar from the crowd a few minutes later drew my attention back again. I turned just in time to see the man running towards my car. He was moving fast, his head tilted as he took huge gulps of air, like a long-distance runner coming up to the home stretch and calling on all his reserves of energy. He was shirtless and his baggy pants flapped like sails on a boat hopelessly out of control as he passed by my window. Behind him came the woman, brandishing a small kitchen knife in her right hand.

The man was glancing behind him as he ran. When the woman's pursuit stalled a few yards behind the car he stopped just in front of the hood and stood there, pacing back and forth, ready to take off in case she started again.

"T'ink yuh can bust mah head an get away wid it, nuh? I goin' fix you up today, just wait and see," she said. "I don' mind going to jail for yuh, you know." As she spoke, she waved the knife in the air and made upward stabbing motions, like a conductor waving a baton.

The man was standing there, his head twisted to the left, looking over his shoulder. He seemed to be trying to gauge the extent of a wound on his back –I could see blood trickling from a cut. He kept checking his wound and alternately taking glances at the woman, like a dog on the lookout for his owner who was seeking to punish him for some transgression.

The woman made several attempts to pursue the man but every time she did, he ran off. Then, she would stop and walk back to her position, and he would return to his. They were like two prize fighters returning to their neutral corner after every round. Eventually, pride and the constant jeering from the crowd seemed to get the better of him and he picked up two small pieces of concrete from some construction debris at the side of the road. As he walked closer to her, she retreated and disappeared into the shack.

The man was now standing no more than two feet

from me and was using the car as a shield. His face was pockmarked all over: on the cheeks, on his broad nose, as if he had never fully recovered from the pox when he was a child. And, he had one of those brutally short haircuts, the type given to inmates of a prison.

When the woman returned a few minutes later she still had the knife, but she was now carrying a small saucepan in her right hand. The saucepan was black with soot and in the haze of the afternoon, vapor rose slowly from the inside.

They both approached my car from opposite directions.

"I gan cut yuh *rass*," she said, waving both the saucepan and the knife at the same time. "Yuh t'ink I scare to go to jail for yuh, nuh? Wait an' see."

In the meantime, the man said nothing, had said nothing through the entire confrontation. Now, he merely weighed the missiles, tossing them up and down in his hands, sending a warning to her. He still took an occasional glance over his shoulder at his wound, as if he had to remind himself of the reason behind the standoff. But most of the time, he flipped those pieces of concrete around and sucked his thick bottom lip into his toothless mouth.

And there I was, sitting in the car, watching Toothless, watching the woman, watching them watch each other, and wondering what I should do. At any moment the action could begin but I couldn't leave the car from the left door since I would be directly in his line of fire and leaving from the right side would make me vulnerable to a steaming pot of the woman's home-made brew.

Then, suddenly, the woman emptied the steaming broth into the gutter and made a hasty dash towards the shack. I wondered what had startled her, or was she going for more weapons?

In a few seconds, I saw the reason for her precipitous action.

As she ran away from the car, a man on a bicycle came up behind her, peddling furiously to catch her before she made it to the shack. The Cyclist caught up with her just outside the shack, jumped off and grabbed her around the waist. He was a big guy, with massive shoulders and long arms that reached out to wrestle the knife and the pot away from her.

“Come on wid me to the police station,” Cyclist said. “You people disturb the peace too many times. Dis nonsense mus' stop.” And, he led her away, taking the evidence with him: the knife, which was now protruding from his back pocket, the pot in his left hand as he pushed the cycle by the handle.

Cyclist and the woman passed Toothless who had discarded his missiles. Now, he stood around, his hands swinging loosely as if he was just casually standing by the roadside, the way so many men in the tropics do in the middle of the afternoon.

The crowd followed closely behind Cyclist, pleading with him to give the woman another chance, that they would keep an eye on her to ensure it did not happen again. After he'd travelled a hundred yards or so, Cyclist relented, gave the knife and pot to someone in the crowd and rode off. The crowd clapped and cheered as the cop went on his way and then Toothless went up to the woman, held her around the waist and steered her towards the shack.

The crowd applauded as Toothless opened the door of the shack for the woman. It was as if the crowd had just witnessed yet another episode in an ongoing drama. And, the last thing I saw before the Toothless and the woman disappeared, was the great smack he placed on her lips and the wide smile of pleasure it brought to her face.

Rex finally returned to the car with his pail of water.
"What was all de commotion about?" He said.
I sighed. "Nothing, just another lovers tryst."

11. BREAKING FREE
by CLIFF RAJKUMAR

Amidst the clutter and the noise, peace,
and harmony awaits the restless mind.

Look beyond the obvious,
every moment is precious and irreplaceable

Be awake and revel in the birth
and empowering energy of the rising sun.

Listen to the harmony of the sound
of silence and invoke your divinity.

Probe deep within, unrestrained,
and experience the spiritual *You.*

Kindness, along with compassion
for the less fortunate strengthens character.

Our imperfections allow our humility
to blossom and facilitate growth.

Judgement is like a rock—once thrown,
it breaks relationships.

Watch the clouds roll by and dream
of boundless possibilities.

The river of time equalizes all things

in the cosmic ocean of pure awareness.

The chatter of small minds will suffocate
you with mind games, if allowed.

Connect with the majestic and healing
power of nature's benevolence.

Break free and soar beyond the limitations
of temporal superficial entrapment

And experience the sublime blissful
self that is the birthright of each soul.

12. HARD EARS PICKNEY
by Shabeena RAMJOHN

Gawd,
Me an' yuh need fi talk,
Cause me mek wan promise seh meh nah go tell nobody.
Today me talk tuh Savitree.
Me notice everday before school bell ring,
She ah buy green mango with salt an' pepper,
She ah eat am till she mouth bun,
And the leh leh leak out,
Den me see she ah cry all de time,
Like she nah know whah old people seh,
When yuh cry yuh ah kill yuh muma and dadee,
So meh ask she by the school pipe *Whah wrong*.

Gawd!
Well whah me go tell yuh,
De hard ears gyal gone an' big she belly fuh ah conductor man.
Meh never leff suh shock yet,
Dem cudda cut me an nah find no blood,
But is truth she ah talk,
Me see she with me own two eye-ball dem,
She ah bus ride whole night an' day,
Suh me nah doubt.
But Gawd whah she guh do,
She nah done school,
An' she done turn baby mudda.

Gawd,
How meh sorry fuh she mudda,

Poor Aunty Pat,
Whole day dah lady ah stan' up in dah hawt hawt sun,
She ah sell de lil bora,
Struggle she ah struggle fuh buy wan uniform.
What guh happen gawd,
Me nah want de baby fuh suffah,
Me always used to tell Savitree nah go wid dah chamar bai!
Me just want fuh tell somebody gawd,
Ah only yuh can help she now.

13. GUYANA'S SEAWALL
by James C. RICHMOND

I know a seawall where love was born
Where love returned and love to scorn
Where dates were made and fell apart again
Like the elusive 'S' of spade in the lovers' game
The seawall where the sky looks big
And eyes alight from within sometimes skid
Knowing not to tender hearts may bring.

The same seawall where I'll love you *Until*
Where I'll love you until death. *Until!*
Sometimes its love fulfilled
And those who love spares, may wait *Until*
To revisit the seawall and love will.

That seawall where as far as I can see
The sea departs
But lovers come with tender hearts
Though muddy deep and wide goes the sea
My love for you will always be
Though morning gone and night by then
My love for you will never end.

14 GRANNY GONE
by Ray WILLIAMS

I never got to know my Grandmother Annie Sobers that well since we seldom visited her home in Chalmers, a neighbourhood on the east side of Georgetown, the capital of Guyana, formerly British Guiana. I however will always remember the day of her funeral in 1950, when I was just seven years old.

That afternoon, watching as my mother Mildred stood weeping over a long brown wooden box placed in the middle of her mother's drawing room, I couldn't help but feel sad for her. I later looked across from where my big sister Pam and I were sitting and wondered: Why would my gray-haired Granny want to sleep in this white satin-frilled box draped in a black skirt resting on two wooden legs?

Several ladies dressed in their 'Sunday best,' of purple, black and white, kept coming up to my mother—whom we called Mammam—to hug and kiss her, yet no one smiled. Seeing this and hoping to make our dear Mammam feel better, Pam and I went over to hold her hand, but expecting a smile as she glanced up, we were met by her watery eyes before she turned and looked down at pale-faced Granny once more.

With all the commotion going on, we expected Granny to at least wake up and ask, "Why in God's name you' all people crying in meh house?"

But she didn't, and after a while I just returned to my seat, disappointed. Aunt Flo, Mamam's older sister, seeing us sulking, soon cheered us up with a cup of tea and a big slice of her delicious yellow sponge cake covered in white icing. Of course, I had to go and spill some tea on my nice new black short pants, but Mamman didn't notice—too busy staring at Granny.

Pam did however, and scolded me saying, "Boy...look what yuh did stupid, yuh lucky yuh didn't stain yuh nice white shirt too."

Off in a corner, a couple of men stood talking and drinking as if they were at a party. That was until a sad-faced man dressed in a black suit walked up and moved everybody, including my dad and my five big brothers away from Granny with a gentle wave of his white-gloved hands. I sat up then to see him next lower a large wooden cover containing a small glass window on top and place it over her in the shiny box. After he screwed it in place and removed the smelly white flowers piled around her, I tiptoed to take a peep and was surprised to find my dear Granny still asleep through it all.

White-painted wooden houses shaded under tall tropical trees crawled by our open window as our procession of black cars drove through the streets of our busy city. Turning several corners, my sister and I sat up, poked our heads out and made faces at the stopped traffic. We knew we were annoying our parents who at first ignored us, preferring to stare forward in silence. But nothing frightened us more than looking further ahead of the procession, towards the leading black horse-drawn carriage driven by a grim-faced man dressed in black coattails and a black top hat, making us quickly pull our heads back in.

Bored with how long the drive was taking, I started to amuse myself by braying at my sister while moving my feet up and down pretending I was prancing like the horses, and even laughed, imitating the clickety clack of their steel-tipped shoes stomping on the paved road. Pam, however, didn't find it amusing, knowing what was coming next.

"Yuh better behave yuh self if yuh know what's good fuh yuh eh boy," she said. That's when my father Walter looked back and glared at me, causing me to sit still from then on.

Along the way, I was surprised to see people on the pavements stopping and staring at the carriage's glass windows, some even making the sign of the cross as we passed. Stranger still, was seeing a couple of men tipping their hats at Granny's flower-draped box as if they knew her.

Soon after entering the gates of La Repentir Cemetery, family and friends gathered around, watching with sad faces as Grannie's box with its nice brown coat of paint reflecting in the fading sunset was slowly lowered into a dark muddy hole in the ground. Afterwards, four men clad in blue dungaree overalls and soiled black rubber boots, first loosened, and then pulled up two lengthy muddied ropes from under her box. With muscles bulging and sweat dripping, they shovelled heaps of rust-coloured mud and small rocks from a nearby mound into the hole, burying Granny's box under its weight. I looked over at my mother whose tears were pouring down even more, and finally realized Granny was indeed going to a different place.

I didn't like what they were doing. though, and worried whether Granny would ever be able to crawl out when she awoke. That's when I moved even closer for a better look as the priest started praying in some strange language I didn't understand. Furthermore, I thought it rude seeing him throwing handfuls of dirt into the hole onto Granny, its clumps of earth landing with a hollow thump. Still curious, I leaned even further, so worried about saving Granny that I didn't at first notice my feet slipping on the wet grass until it was too late, and started screaming at the top of my lungs.

With arms flailing, trying my best to catch on to any and everything, I closed my eyes expecting any second to crash to the bottom. In the nick of time, a strong hand reached out and grabbed me.

"Don't worry son, yuh won't fall in, just hold onto me from now on yuh hear?" And although my father held me close while consoling me, dripping in perspiration I still couldn't stop my knees from shaking. Through blurry eyes I bravely looked down again, wondering whether Granny really wanted me to join her in that different place, but without hesitation held onto my dad even tighter knowing that although I loved my Granny dearly, with darkness casting long ominous shadows across nearby tombstones, the only place I truly wanted to be right then, was home.

NOSTALGIA

15. SHIVANI WEDS
by Habeeb ALLI

Knowing her journey
From Guyana to Montreal
She finds Faith in God
That lead her to Allah, for real.

The Princess of her mother
Weds the beau from Sri Lanka.
While the journey has been uphill
Today she finds joy in her love
like Rumi poetry

So kind and generous
Always finding in her heart to donate kindly,
Loving her children immensely
Hisham has found a lady of his dreams,
just here in Brampton beautifully

Like Koti roti and dhallpuri
Cuisines from two cultures
With a single Faith, like a river
with two tributaries. When the bells ring,
this will be a match made in Paradise, you'll see!

16. SAPODILLA GRINS
by Jerome BRANCHE

sapodilla's bark is grim
for slim
nine-year-old shins
that would reach beyond the
glories
of jack
him of the bountiful beans
stalk of satisfaction

sapodilla's bean
black and brilliant
against their honeybed of taste
frame the tenderest temptation
which must age first
to give satisfaction

the sapodilla muse
would refuse
ogres and englishmen
she said instead
eat this

17. LOVE
by Alicia DANIELS

Love is like fire deep in your soul,
Love is like God because it never grows old,
It's an ingredient in the batter of life,
So important that it casts out strife.

Love can build bridges,
Love can build hope,
Love can lift a disillusioned heart and
make it float.

Wherever you be, look to see
The many little places where love can be.

18. WE ARE OLDER NOW
by Francis Quamina FARRIER

Comrades, we were there when the bombs exploded,
when the shots were fired. When the babies died.
We were young then, and to us it seemed like fun.
But we are older now and are seeking our place in the sun.

We look back to those days
when the sky was reddened with the glow
of buildings ablaze with the fires of hate,
quenched only with the tears of grief
of those who dearly wanted peace.
Souls were degenerated to the bottomless pit
while their bodies dared to breathe
the pure air of this earthly paradise.

Comrades, we were young and we were there
when the police threw tear-gas
and we laughed while we choked
because the police were our playmates
and it was fun. But we are older now and seek jobs.
But the big men who begged us to save their
buildings from the destruction
have destroyed the memory of our gallantry.

Comrades, we remember the days
when our brother sat at the gate
of the governor's house, a black sash across his chest

covering his grieving heart, the distant future in his eyes
a soundless plea on his lips to save his people
from a fate worse than death.

You remember, Comrades, how we offered
sympathetic stares at our brother?
We were young then and did not know
that the fuse would have been lit, and the explosion
would have sent scores to their graves.

We are older now, Comrades
and pray God, it will never happen again.

19. THAT WE COULD BE NEWBORN
by Lisa FREEMANTLE

January 6, 2021

That we could be newborn;
No brush strokes of bias or scorn
but colour-blinded,
not narrow-minded

That we could live newborn;
No bigotry or misinformation,
Instead, a lack of intolerant discrimination.
Without partiality and prejudgment
forced in steps before you walk.
Without unfair and prejudicial words
put in mouths before you talk

That we could feel newborn;
Bask in the warmth of the sun, pure clean light.
Know that all agree on what's wrong and right.
Untouched by slanted and swayed deceptions,
Our slates wiped free of any marks of preconceptions

That we could sense newborn;
Envision all minds uncluttered by ego, spoil and greed,
Shared resources for everyone, nobody in need.
Our canvasses clear
Our lives lived without fear.

That we could be reborn…

...To a world of innocence and acceptance by all.
Where differences celebrate and stand up tall.
Where welcomes are friendly and never cold.
Where wars find no purchase, evils no grip to hold.
Where hope lives for a brighter world view.
Where ingenuity is unfettered and love is too.

That we could be newborn...

20. TOWARDS THE PEBBLED SHORE
by Peter JAILALL

(For Edwin)

When I heard my friend Edwin died
I was sipping coffee at the Hilton hotel
In far-away Montego Bay,
I put down the cup
Walked to the beach
Alone.

I sat under a swaying coconut tree
Watching the waves roll in.
And Shakespeare's Sonnet LX came to mind:
'Like as the waves make towards the pebbled shore
So do our minutes hasten to their end.'
Closing my eyes-
Memories rolled in with the waves-
Like the day when I collapsed
At the breakfast table in Jamaica
How Edwin and Indrani rushed to my side.

Today, I'm so far away
I cannot kiss dear Edwin's forehead
For the last time.
The pebbles roll ashore in
The waves' sorrowful sonnet,
When will death roll in for me?
Where will that be?
And who will be there to meet me
At the pebbled shore?

21. THROWING A HUMMINGBIRD
by Ian McDONALD

My study window overlooks the garden,
a branch of bougainvillea trails upwards –
within my reach this last month.
This morning, a hummingbird tangled in it,
fluttered and fell on to my desk,
stunned and still. I seized it quick.
I swear I felt its beating heart,
saw closer than I ever will again
the soft green feathers at its breast.
Threw that green-gold shred of light
soaring flashing heavenwards again.
This happened once in eighty years.
These lines make no particular point.
Just if any reader sees them,
they might suggest that everything
is miracle and mystery all one's life.

22. TRAILS OF TREASURES
by Janet NAIDU

No so long ago,
roses whispered the gentle song of your name,
and your mother held you close
in her arms, her eyes and heart listening.
Her garden widened with sunflowers
across promises of a fragrant future
like a vessel at harbor—
with every comfort for the journey.

I slip into memory
and catch your enduring years
in a basket of floral keepsakes—
a birth marks a mother's grace
like a velvet sky at nightfall, looming.
Every glance unfolds another moment
captured by the boldness of wings,
by the freshness of paintings.

The soft pull of eastern drums
echo and warm your heart,
like an infant on its mother's bed.
The sun follows you through the fields
where your name is planted, grown
among the women, girls too
adorned in colourful head ties.
Their grass knives swing in the sun
cutting new grass without malice.

But their moments cannot pass

without the wild songs and rhymes
that ring of lessons in pride: of survival
in the way some work shortens play.

Your heart missed a privilege,
only fingertips away
where skipping ropes and hopscotch
swelled in girlish giggles.
Not even a day of A and B or C
made it your way—but pages at night,
not even another alphabet, in your veins—
but eastern languages at wasteland.
Still, not one leftover book,
shortened pencil
or unmatched ribbons in your hair
for only a day.

I hear the penalty in your voice,
deep void as your head leaned
against the school—in the yard alone,
hiding your face from the rain.
There, you glimpsed a pressed uniform,
girls ten years or so, clapping a rhyme.
The small of the window left you gazing
into the ways of the school room.
But the grass bundle you carried
remained at your feet, waiting.

Each sunrise caressed your steps
across the long distances
in weight upon your head

Now, I walk with you—in your hand,

along the length of your feet
carrying the unwritten words
in my heart.

I feel your time—your golden heart
hiding its silent wish—to read.
Our nights move, slowly receding
long after the sun closes her door.
your gentle walk nurtures my spirit,
In a way, like a waterfall
constant, voluminous in flow.
Still, like a sunburst,
your eyes smile a thousand gifts.

From the collection “Winged Heart” (Greenheart, 1999)
In dedication to my late mother Chelema Naidu (nee Murugan)

23. CURE-FOH-AAL
by Petamber PERSAUD

we didn mine (twice, sing song rhythm)
a bungie
from a haad baal
nor a bran'
from a coconut-branch bat

we didn mine (twice, sing song rhythm)
cartwheeling
an faaling flat pon we baak, brakz
nor doing belly-buss, blash-ii
wen we plunge in de punt trench

we didn mine
raiding wet fruit tree in de night
an geh bruise up an hairy worm in we tail

we didn mine laaning fuh ride bicycle
And laaning lil boy bicycle nah gah brakes
spring-jump and miss de saddle
tow gal pon bicycle bar and geh vd

we didn mine (twice, sing song rhythm)
getting beat up black an blue
laas day foh school
playing fiah fiah bun mih han
or telling we parents a bareface lie
an getting licks like peas
wid belna an broom

kaz at de end
was a solid glass of suga-wata
ole people cure
cure-foh-aal
cure foh aal lil chil'ren ruckionness (repeat chorus going off stage....)

24. I AM WHO I AM
by Ken PUDDICOMBE

I am from Guyana.
Once called British Guiana.
The Land Of Many Waters and
the towering Kaieteur.

I am the sum total of generations
who came long before I took my first breath.
I am the product of east meets west.

The descendant of people from
far-away lands who found
their way to an unknown country,
seeking a better life.

They came from England
and took over plantations from the Dutch.
They were overseers, part of the
white Plantocracy. The people who enforced
the Indentureship laws.
Saw that the sugar estate
ran efficiently and made profits
for the absentee landlord in England
sipping his tea sweetened with sugar
made from cane grown in
British Guiana. Along with Demerara
Rum for the mighty English navy
sailing the seven seas,
ruling an empire where
the sun never set.

They also came from India and worked
the land for those white plantation owners
in England and Scotland. They grew the cane,
cut it at harvest time, filled the punts,
went home to their garden plots
to supplement their piece wage.

They were planters, cane cutters, stackers
weeders. They worked in the fields
and in the factory. They lifted and heaved.
They walked with bundles
balanced on their head.

And somewhere
along the way a lineage was created
including me along with many others.

*

They braved a long voyage across the sea.
They worked long hours in the blazing tropical sun.
They survived and built a home away from home.

I am the product of east meets west.
For better or worse, that's who I am.
I am grateful to the pioneers who left their homeland.
And I don't pass judgment.

Because, if they hadn't come,
where would I be, today?

25. CHERISH LIFE
By Cliff RAJKUMAR

In an endless sea of absolute desolation
Amidst galaxies, stars and black holes,
A solitary pine tree clings to life
On the edge of a death-defying precipice

Embracing the glorious sun.
Braving the fearless wind.
Welcoming the life-giving rain.

Such is the benevolence of Mother Earth.
Why then waste this precious gift of life?
With all the glorious wonders still to discover,
And purposes yet to fulfil.

Contained in this tiny speck of life-giving sand,
Is a phenomenon—a cyclical cosmic dance
Happening each moment, within the realm
of time and existence.

Be grateful—wake up and cherish
life's conscious awareness
For our mortal end is only a breath away.

This human manifestation of our spiritual being is a rare gift,
Celebrate life, choose to be happy,
spread joy and embrace all.

For, we are the masters of our fate and destiny.

26. THE SWORDSWOMAN
by Shabeena RAMJOHN

From the murky depths of the Berbice River
she rose, Wielding more than her sword.

A woman not defined by the ties of tradition,
Her mindset leaving behind the expectations
of Great Britain.

Dropping the veil,
Her slender neck,
The rise and fall of her chest
with every determined breath,

Brown nipples taste like sweet sapodillas.

On toned legs she took her fighting stance,
With pride she wore her crown,
Her skin the combination of two races.

Standing on wet sand,
Villagers passing by made disgusted faces,
She worried not for she felt her ancestors' embraces,
She was a resident of the Ancient county,
Her beauty certainly not the only bounty.

27. WHERE POMEROON MEETS
by James RICHMOND

Down the river Essequibo
Where the Pomeroon meets?
To get my pot of Gold
My journey to complete.
Under the shores like men of yore
Toiling in the sun and heat.
Of this blessed earth
My melodic songs will seek.
Like poetry and the reverent hymn
With reverence meek.
I bow my mud-caked feet
On the ground that my God did speak.
And shout to the heavens:
My Eldorado I found which men seek.

To journey home along my rivers banks and caves
My vivid dream and my Cinderella will come.
To talk in lofty phrase
Of my travels and things I've seen. Under the
moon-lit sky of the days
Bringing to life a newborn. To the essence of life,
one's left amazed
And the things that men found can never be heaven
bound. And craved. Like food to return to the
Pomeroon.
To refill the vision of all age.

All sons and daughter will journey too. And always will
remain in Guyana's heartland. Where from the bosom

remembers again
Even in solitude and distant lands.
And will hasten to bring fame
To my Beloved Mother or Father.
My heart-felt love, a heart which bled in pain
Demerara, Berbice, Essequibo where the Pomeroon
meets. Guyana remains!

28. ESCAPE FROM ROBBEN ISLAND
by Ray WILLIAMS

Sunday morning's gray skies hovered above majestic Table Mountain as our crowded high-speed ferry bobbed and weaved at the mercy of the turbulent Indian Ocean during our forty-five-minute crossing.

With my wife Margaret and our tour group seated safely inside, feeling somewhat adventurous, I stepped out to the open deck, and finding a sturdy railing held on for dear life. Salty spray peppered my face watching large whitecap waves lashing against the stern, and as picturesque Cape Town on the mainland faded further into the background, ever so often I'd turn and look at the once foreboding Robben Island looming large in the distance and feel my anxiety increasing by the minute.

It was May 23rd. 2004, the last day of our awe-inspiring vacation in beautiful South Africa. Travelling from Johannesburg, for days we had toured several picturesque cities and townships including the capital Pretoria. Photographing a variety of animals in their natural habitat on our safari in Kruger Park was quite breathtaking. Some in the group even got quite tipsy indulging in delicious wine tasting visiting several vineyards; and trekking to the tip of the Cape of Good Hope—the southernmost point in Africa—was a dream come true. And finally, we delighted in the splendour of multicultural Cape Town, the city known as the 'Jewel in the crown.' But we knew however, we couldn't leave without paying homage to the memory of their benevolent President Nelson Rolihlahla Mandela, and therefore felt duty-bound to make this visit.

Upon arrival, I disembarked on wobbly legs and stinging lungs triggered by the cool salty sea air and accompanied our small Canadian tour group towards our waiting coach to traverse the grounds of this once insufferable leper colony—turned penal institution.

Standing outside the coach as we approached was our tour guide, a short, gray-bearded East Indian man with a voice still pained. He informed us he was a former political prisoner with Mr. Mandela, and in describing the hardships they endured as we drove past gleaming limestone quarries, I couldn't help but envision the former inmates wielding pickaxes in the blistering sun; eyes red from the glare, muscles sore and weary, drenched in sweat as they hammered away. Around the next bend stood a green-domed mosque with multi-coloured flags at the gate flapping in the wind, soon followed by a series of one-storied, gray-stone barracks which once served as the prisoner's dormitories.

Leaving the coach and our able tour guide, as I neared the red-roofed building my legs suddenly felt quite weighted down; my face damp, and out of concern I purposely began lagging behind. It's then it dawned on me I was about to walk in the painful footsteps of those unfortunate prisoners who for years endured brutal and dehumanizing treatment in opposing the generational apartheid political system. But I couldn't lag for long since a tall strapping black man standing at the door dressed in a dark blue gym suit waved us in with a broad smile. He too, was another prison companion who'd served time in his teens and has since gained great redemption sharing his anguish and story with the world.

We crowded onto long wooden benches lining dull white concrete walls, and while listening to his compassionate voice I kept scanning the room, noticing among other things a few remaining double-bunked beds stacked in the far corner. Painted on the wall between the beds, still visible though quite faded, remained a small mural of the Christ figure. Thoughts of it being their sacred space came to mind, no doubt giving hope and courage to those inmates who gazed upon it daily and yet carried on.

Tears welled up among our group when our guide went on to describe in painful detail their daily routine. “The guards woke us up at five each morning,” he said, with a cracking voice. "Imagine, how difficult it was jostling others, no privacy, just trying to use our small stinking and overcrowded bathroom all at once. What’s worse was those unfortunate late comers, they got sent to solitary confinement for several days for not being ready.” He paused to compose himself while pacing the floor, "Imagine, no heat in the winter, yet we had to brave the cold dressed in short pants and short-sleeved shirts, which was our uniform all year long, you know. We had to huddle to stay warm sleeping on flimsy straw mats on these same damp and cold concrete floors in our dormitories and cells. It should come as no surprise to you that through the years many of us developed long-lasting health problems.” He further made it clear, as we suspected, the prison officials did little to alleviate their pain, seeing them mainly as sub-humans, and the political activists like Mandela as terrorists.

Out into the ‘Big Yard’ we followed, and by then the sun had peeped out, warming our sympathetic souls somewhat. It was here the future President of South Africa and others, sat without shelter, breaking rocks for hours under the watchful eyes of their unforgiving Afrikaans guards. There was great camaraderie and respect among the confined, the guide explained, and as a result, their leader Nelson Mandela, fondly called Madiba, managed to secretly write and conceal the manuscript of his acclaimed autobiography—"*Long walk to freedom*."

Across from the 'Big Yard' I noticed a range of cell blocks with bar-encased windows looking out onto its rectangular confines. Our guide then informed us one of the cells in this section B, was that of Mr. Mandela. Without hesitation, like children outside a candy store, we rushed through the main door, anxious to view what has since become his shrine.

Prisoner 46664 resided in cell number 5 since arriving in 1964, where he remained for the first eighteen of his twenty-seven years of incarceration. It was through the bars of those soiled glass panes he viewed the world and methodically defined his destiny.

I was in no hurry though, so I watched and waited as Margaret and the other members of our excited group jostled and shifted places trying to get a better view and photo of his faded, blue-coloured cell. As I'd done on past trips, wanting to take photos unhindered while having my quiet moment with the memories still lingering, I'd usually stand by until they were all done and walking away, before taking up my position.

Between the locked door and window of his eight by seven-foot cell, I pictured Madiba traversing almost the distance of the circumference of the world several times. Carving a well-worn path, he must've been careful not to step on his thin-layered straw mattress lying on the concrete floor to the right, nor the covered red slop bucket serving as a toilet in the left corner. Between photos, I grabbed the iron bars of his door for a while as he'd done countless times, hoping to connect and feel what it was like being on the other side.

Within minutes, as if in a graveyard, eerie silence descended on the long hallway. I stopped filming and looked up and down the worn concrete floor, seeing only the bars of the cell doors casting their lengthy shadows in the dim light. Where had the other members of the tour group all gone, I wondered, and where was my wife, why didn't she tell me when they were leaving?

We had been informed our time on the island was limited, since we had to board the early afternoon ferry back to Cape Town. I began to worry, thinking if I didn't catch up with the group, now on their way to the boat, I'd also miss our bus to the airport and the flight that evening back home to Canada, via England.

Trying to think clearly while supressing my fears, my breath came in gasps, heart pounded against my chest, and cold sweat dampened my brow. Looking around, I could already feel the harrowed ghosts from every cell of Robben Island closing in on me. Images of abuse, starvation, insanity and suicide still resonating within those dreaded walls swirled through my head. I had to get out of there, and fast. Suddenly, feeling like an involuntary prisoner, I took off down the dimly lit hallway heading towards the first big door I saw. Screeching to a halt, I yanked open the heavy steel door and poked my head in, but neither heard nor saw any of the group. Where could they be I wondered, as the eerie silence prevailed?

Almost frantic now, I looked around and saw three other brown steel doors ahead of me. No time to waste—I had to make a quick decision. That's when I took a chance, allowing the child in me to point, saying, "Eenie, meenie, minee, moe," before grabbing the handle of the nearest door. I'd no sooner stuck my head in when I saw yet another door a few feet away. Time was my enemy; I had to go for broke. Sweat clung to my shirt as I turned the knob on this other door and glanced to my right. There thankfully, I saw the heel of a woman's black shoe as she was just about to head through another door.

Holding back the tears, I followed her out into the main courtyard, past the sparse cacti plants and low shrubbery, leading to the main gate over which a large painted sign read—*Robbeneiland*—with the caption—*We serve with pride.* I had no time nor desire to laugh at its sad and hypocritical irony, but started running along the path towards the dock where in the distance I soon spotted Margaret and the rest of our group walking towards the waiting boat moored alongside the port.

"Margaret...Margaret...how come you didn't wait for me?" I said panting, after catching up.

"Well, you always like to stay behind and take photos," she said with a grin, as we got in line. "Of course, you knew what time the boat was leaving, but no—you always want to have your way, so why should I bother calling you, since you'd ignore me anyhow taking all your pictures, and furthermore..."

Boarding the ferry, I peered beyond the far horizon, seeing the imposing Table Mountain sitting in full sunlight. And as we sailed out into the now calm Indian Ocean, I kept counting my blessings in appreciation of the relentless courage and sacrifices made by Nelson Mandela and his numerous fellow prisoners. Yet I couldn't help but admit harping back on my recent scare, in comparison, Madiba would've laughed.

YEARNINGS

29. BIBI LEAVES ON THE WINGS OF LOVE

by Habeeb ALLI

With such a shock
Too soon, with a miracle between
You have taken our breath away
Leaving a trail of grieving families and friends faraway.

Understood that you were in pain.
Accepted you bid farewell with restraint
With that smiling face
Always caring for Faith and the human race.

On the two wings of love
You sail, unbroken
Unto the heavens like a dove,
Strengthening us while showing compassion

We know the angels are singing
Songs that marked the dash between life and freedom.
Prayers you prayed, whilst we kept hoping
Are now answered in God's infinite wisdom.

Healing like a scarred wound

Is how a mother remembers her daughter every sound
And what we yearn for
Is that spirit of volunteering you are so cherished for!

Rest In Power, Bibi Raqeea Mohamed

30. REFLECTIONS (FOR MLD)
by Jerome BRANCHE

after a time
it was just the dreams
floating dreams
with wavy weeds
and nervous fish flushing through
in a hurry

flying dreams with
heavy wings deep green valleys
below
and a highway stretching into the distance
towards a nervous hiding place
of hastily clasped hands
and worried whispers

at heart it was
the Friday nights though
stretching
like a highway
stacking up like loosened panes
from your jalousie window
until the house had none

there is no life
in a living room without
windows
open to the wind the rain

and after a time it

became clear
it was the absence
it was the absence that made the heart
grow somber

31. FRAGILE
by Alicia DANIELS

It's amazing how we can put pen to paper,
To highlight a scourge,
Potentially helping our women and girls
to live safer.

Day after day, year after year,
So many suffer and die silently in fear
and without care.

We see it in the statistics,
Seventy percent of females forced or
coerced into this shady business.

Imagine, in the midst of wanting a better life,
Many daughters, sisters, friends are
shackled to this vice,

Some, deceived into thinking they've
found a way to a better day,
Instead, treated as slaves with little to no pay.

Like fragile pieces of glass or pottery,
Mishandled, abused, subjected to Poverty.

Ready to jump off the brink of insanity.
It's time **T**rafficking **I**n **P**ersons (TIP)
is brought into plain sight,

From under the darkness of twilight.

No society is perfect, we admit
But we must work together to eliminate TIP.

In a season of brazen crimes,
Don't let our diamonds be peddled for dimes.

Let my humble words in your ear resonate,
Don't let another woman or girl suffer
the same fate,

Be each other's keeper as the Good
Book reads,
So that together, we rid society of these
evil deeds.

32. A LITTLE DROP OF WATER
by Francis Quamina FARRIER

I am a drop of water, way high up in the sky.
A little drop of water, I sure am getting by,
Way, way above your planet, just having my own way.
But soon I'll be an ocean, I sure will have my say.
A little drop of water, within a cloud so black,
With many other raindrops, we all will soon attack.

A little drop of water, so small and high above.
With many, many others, and flying like a dove.
A little drop of water, I'll soon be plunging down,
From way above your planet, that's going round and round.
Where live so many people, who need us every day,
I am so proud to help them, to live and have a say.

A little drop of water, with millions more I see,
About to fall as raindrops, a mighty force are we.
We're just a little shower, yet a mighty force we are.
We come to give you life, no matter near or far.

Now here we are a shower, a-plunging to the earth.
Somewhere within a forest, to give it some re-birth.
We need to know this forest, this pristine place we see.
We drip between the foliage,
Oh, what a place to be!

I am a drop of water, now here upon the earth.
Within a pristine forest, now dripping down to earth.
Within this pristine forest, here in a land down south.

Not far from the equator, I do not have a doubt.
With many other raindrops, fresh from the falling rain.
We group around each other, to find an easy lane.

Now, there's a path, we've found it,
That goes beyond the hill.
Into a creek so pretty, and ready for our fill.
These million tiny raindrops, from high above the
earth.
Now part of Nature's Cycle, to give the land rebirth.
And also give to humans, that needed liquid life.
To man and also woman, to mister and his wife.

So here we go a-flowing, along a trodden path.
Within this pristine forest, with pleasure and no wrath.
A million little rain drops, clear shining like the sun.
We know what we're doing, we're having so much fun!

A million little raindrops, now building up a force.
With many million others, we're following a course.
Set eons, years before us, we're following a path.
That leads from this old mountain, to valleys and a
bath.

I am a drop of water, now strong as I could be.
Someone has just informed me, that I will be a sea.
That mighty ships will sail on, for pleasure and for gain.
A sea that's named Caribbean, like blood within some
veins.

So here we go together, towards that sea you know.
In this enormous cycle, from sky to earth we flow.
From me and many others, down to that sea we go,
In face of that great Tradewind, that southernly do

blow.

The creek has now gone wider, and certainly we see.
That it is now a river, and wider it will be.
As we are joined by others, we certainly will find,
That one, then ten, and millions more, will wind.

Our path around the hills and mountains tall,
We skip and jump, over rapid and waterfall.
It's so much fun, as we stay together,
Be it sunny and calm or be it stormy weather.

Our journey goes on, but there's something wrong.
We're caught up in what looks not like where we were born.
High up in the sky, so clean and pure,
And all living creatures can endure.

Now there's mud, there is silt, there is mercury, too!
And all living creatures, have become so few!
While men with greed, earn wealth galore!
Men who seem to have no heart or soul.
They dig and they defile the earth so pure,
And pollute the rivers just to secure
Gold and diamonds and minerals rich.
As they poison and kill out every single fish.

A little drop of water, so pure from above.
And healthy and bright as a turtle dove.
My friends and I, now tinted with grief,
Of men who need to have rich minerals as their feed.

Oh, what a shame, oh, what a disgrace!
To pollute the earth and its beautiful face.
The gold they mine, and the wealth that they gain,

Is such a grief for this fallen rain.

I've come to the earth to share the joy,
With every man, woman, girl and boy.
But to see the rivers which I help to fill,
Polluted and defiled, is such an ill.

But we'll flow right on, ten trillion of us.
Right on to the ocean, as we certainly must.
We do our part as we promised the Sky.
Even in anger, we must get by.

We hope and we pray, that one bright day,
As you and others have your say,
That mankind will stop this terrible thing
Of defiling the earth and plundering.

I'm a little drop of water, from high up in the sky.
Now in this lovely river, I'm simply passing by.
I've seen the deeds of many evil men.
With untold riches and acumen.

They destroy the land, they take the wealth.
Never minding the future and the people's health.
I'm on my way, but when I return.
Will this land be here, or in an urn?

33. THE EVOLUTION OF RAIN
by Lisa FREEMANTLE

June 7, 2020

Drip, drip, drip...drop!

The Infant:
Teasing source of greenery trickle
Drizzly dewy wetness tickle
Spitting, patter, napping
Tentative tiny lapping
Germinate

The Child:
Playing impish in pools and puddles
Dawdling droplets, muddy cuddles
Splashing innocent foliage flow
Plantlets sprouting; time to grow
Frolic

The Adolescent:
Cocky stormy gush cloudbursts
Torrential tempers, stamp, loud firsts!
Driving drench; no license yet
Swishing, sashaying all just wet
Maturing

The Parent:
Cleansing dirt filled earthy floor
Quenching younglings, gently pour

Patient nurture propagate
Proudly view new life create
Mother-Nature

The Senior:
Sleepy seepage
Old vines creepage
Irregular dabbling
Incoherent babbling
Dribble

All drowsy dowse…
Time for rest…

Drip, drip, drip…drop!

34. FINAL HOUR
by Peter JAILALL

On the end of life's journey
When I am ready to die
Please don't let me die alone
Lying in some sterilized home -
A fearful, cold place
Covered in stiff, bleached bedsheets
Under the glare of fluorescent light
With strangers pulling screens to peep at me
Urging me to die quickly.

Let me die peacefully
In the comfort of my own home
With one bright candle burning by my bedside
My head nestled in my favourite pillow.

Please,
Don't be afraid of me
Come, come closer
Sit beside me
Sing to me
Recite my favourite poem - my *Ajah*
Make me smile
Give thanks for the days I've spent on Earth
Place a drop of water on my warm, dry tongue
With that same old coffee spoon
We used to stir life's mornings away.

Comb my hair
With those loving, slender fingers
Wait with me awhile

Keep watch until death comes
And lull me into a long, deep peaceful sleep.

35. GOING AWAY
by Ian McDONALD

Where my life has been sweetly centred,
this garden is wildfire, sometimes hot and
gold,
ripe-sun-lit blaze of flowers, sky aflame.
This evening colour calmed to mists of lightest blue;
I sit alone in this green and quiet place.
Over the sea wall, far-out grey clouds
merge with silver blush-smudged sea,
white-winged birds, pale shadows,
weave patterns in the darkening air.
Tomorrow I leave here for a while.
Fine drops of rain begin to fall. I won't move
until the hummingbirds appear,
bright jewels gleaming in the dying light,
branch of crystals shaking in the gloom.
When will I return? These days nothing is
certain.

36. THE MAN IN THE PENTHOUSE
by Janet NAIDU

One year later, as he gazed at the sky from his Penthouse condo, wearing his morning robe, Martin Major noticed something different in his life. He had confided in his close friends—on lengthy telephone conversations—that he would never get married again. “I can go it alone, do for myself and live without attachments,” he prided himself. “Now that the warm breeze is rushing near, I won’t need a hand to hold or a woman’s body to warm me over. I have my own beating heart.”

His wife of nearly thirty years had turned him down for a reconciliation. Martin remembered her last words, “You can’t use me for sex anymore!” as she slammed her bedroom door in his face. After some deep thinking, Martin had decided he would pursue a spiritual life.

He explained to his children, “I am leaving everything up to God!” They rarely called him and even ignored his birthday; but he continued to do his ‘duty’—as he liked to reinforce—to pay for their education at University. He sent them emails about his bank deposits into their accounts, just as his parents had done for him. “You must come to see my fantastic view from the Penthouse,” he told his daughters, but so far, no response.

His children had taken their mother’s side and now, after several months, the sky over Lake Ontario seemed grayer. In the southwest corner, over the office tower, a dark patch of clouds hovered closer, threatening a rainy day. He imagined workers hurrying up Bay Street from Union Station, carrying leather cases and heavy backpacks, and freshly brewed coffee from Starbucks. Martin felt he too must hurry. There were expectations for him to write his lectures for a new job at the University, a scheduled appointment with his cardiologist, and his desire for something different in life. He wondered how his day would unfold.

It was midmorning. A sudden burst of cloud sent rain pouring down and clinging at his wide window before rippling, as if the building wept. He saw glimpses of his former life with his wife. He figured that she must have gotten tired of him over the years, too, recalling how he had betrayed her with his two affairs. Even though Martin had ended them, she refused to forgive him and insisted on keeping him distant. For one year, they had slept in separate bedrooms, and hardly communicated except for their children's interests. Occasionally, he enamored her for an entire week with fresh roses and nice words before he ventured into her bedroom for an evening's closeness, only to be rejected.

Soon, they will be divorced.

His view was blurred even as the rain decreased, and now he closed the ivory satin drapery. On the shelf were books on political science, poetry and world's religion. He knew his needs were deeper.

Martin got dressed and took the elevator to Azalia Honeycomb's suite in the building, to see if he could first pay her a friendly visit, but no one answered. Azalia worked at the bank in Customer Services — *perhaps I could stop by and say hello*. He had met her at the poolside a few times. For today, he thought, *I would open an account. Then she will learn something about my status and I will let things evolve.* Somehow he felt safe with Azalia. When they chatted at the swimming pool the previous week, she had shared with him that she too would never remarry. Martin felt touched that Azalia showed him a degree of trust. The surface of the pool water had little waves from the wind when she told him her husband was mentally abusive, how he discounted her ideas, hardly asked about her day and never acknowledged her part in making dinners for his family gathering.

Martin had also shared his pain with Azalia—about his wife's spiritual bankruptcy—how he knew it was written in the books from birth that they must part. He knew she was too worldly and after more than two decades of putting up with her flamboyance and excessiveness, the pillars would collapse. He had warned her that if she did not change, especially with the children in their teens—if she could not walk with him on a quiet, spiritual path and be the devoted wife, he would leave her. Martin crossed his arms and envisioned—*At age fifty-five, even with my heart bypass, my neat salt and paper hair, strong muscles and flat stomach, I can still start over.*

He sensed that Azalia could be that spiritual friend he longed for.

The afternoon sun flooded his room with golden overtones as if welcoming something new. Martin hurried out of his Penthouse. He looked straight ahead in the empty elevator speeding to ground level. He was anxious. But anxious for what? To see Azalia? His impending medical test result? A visit from his children?

Shading from the light drizzle with his umbrella, Martin walked up Bay Street, towards the bank where Azalia worked. He noticed his Cardiologist, Dr. Alan Highgate walking towards him on the way to the hospital.

"Hi Doc!" Martin said.

"Hi Martin, I'll see you at our four o'clock appointment."

"Yes, yes!" Martin walked faster, his unzipped Spring jacket flapping in the wind. His heart thumped and his face flushed. *Gee, I so long to see Azalia, I almost forgot my appointment!*

At the bank, he completed the deposit slip and waited in line. Azalia's bronze complexion and glazed brown eyes captivated him.

In the British Virgin Islands, Azalia had been in a beauty pageant, singing Lulu's "To Sir with Love" for her talent. She had hoped to become an actor, but her father's diplomatic post to Canada changed Azalia's dream. She had to start life all over, working and studying financial investments part-time. She spent many years healing from her broken marriage. Martin felt a sudden deep affection for her. God knows he could fall head over heels. He sensed she had led a spiritual life and maybe at last, she may be the one to bring him some peace.

"Oh, Hello Martin! I didn't know you bank here!" Azalia said.

"I don't. I now want to open a savings account here. Can you deposit this amount for me?" He placed the deposit slip on the counter—the large amount prominent. He hoped she would notice that, despite his impending divorce, he could afford some things in life. He could even take a woman out for more than dinner!

Azalia glanced at the slip, looked into his deep brown eyes, and pointing to a row of offices at the far end of the bank said, "For an amount that large, Martin, you need to see a Financial Advisor over there."

Martin nodded and smiled.

Azalia said, "Anyway, I guess you'll be going to the pool tonight?"

Martin straightened his tie, decorated with rows of ruby-red hearts and held in place with a gold tie clip. His eyes twinkled mischievously. "Oh yes, I'm planning on it. But, do you have time for a coffee on your break?"

"I already took my break. Perhaps another time?" Azalia said.

"Okay."

Martin hurried over to the Financial Advisor, thinking his status didn't matter anymore. What mattered was his honesty. He thought Azalia would appreciate such quality, especially in a man. She would not care that he was a professor, that he had some property and money and could afford to take a woman to a theatre or dinner, or even something grand like a trip overseas. Maybe she would be one of those women who didn't mind a man with children he still supported. She too could devote her life to serving God. He smiled, imagining Azalia as more his type. He had only met two younger women at poolside who seemed keen for marriage and children. He was done with that.

Azalia was forty-five, attractive with a permanent deep tan. Her brown eyes held a sincere care for the downtrodden as if she'd rescue a poor soul in need. Appearing much younger than her years, perhaps because she had no longer been burdened with a husband, or children to drain her, she had no wrinkles. Her eyes radiated a gentle harmony like a spring vine that could easily wrap around the thickest oak tree. He imagined her in a few years, wearing an elegant gown in his penthouse, be more than a friend and yet welcoming her own room for privacy and independence. By then too, he would be deep into the spiritual journey and there would be no ropes around his neck, like marriage held, no loud music and endless parties from which he ran. He could share truth, love, peace and liberation, all the joyful spirit as in his dreams when he was a boy growing up in Nova Scotia.

He opened his account and felt a sudden rush of hope. *I could be with her. I could see her again tomorrow*.

Half an hour later, while he was relaxing and looking through the window in his Penthouse, the sky was brighter and dark clouds had moved eastward. When the phone rang, the rain had stopped, and Martin saw a light shimmering through the clouds.

"Dad? How are you? How was your doctor's

appointment?"

"Okay, I guess," he said, surprised that his son had contacted him at last. *I was right, I knew my son would come around eventually.*

"When will I see you, Terry?" he said.

"Oh, I don't know dad. The days are getting shorter before I return to university. Anyway, how was your test result?"

"Oh, that. I don't know as yet. When are you going to come around to see my Penthouse? And bring the girls too."

"Well, I'll see. Maybe I'll come around next week. But I can't speak for Lisa and Lara. You know how they hate heights."

"They are big girls now. I can tell they are still mad at me, taking sides. Oh well, what can I do?"

Martin felt his daughters could take a long time to come around, and God only knows, maybe never. He made a wry face and rubbed his hand across his forehead. It was soaking wet. Should he go to see Dr. Alan Highgate or postpone hearing the news? His heart sank some more. Was he trying to escape from something thickening inside him, maybe something going around in huge circles, like a windmill? He would think about it later.

Martin spent much of his time pondering his impending divorce and his heart condition. Would he have to have another bypass? His ever-increasing solitude made him restless.

In the early evening, he went to the swimming pool as usual and after ten laps, he did not see Azalia. She must have changed her mind. He thought of making a promise—one he could keep—that he would forget women, even as friends. *They are not worth investing one's wealth in, one's spiritual strength. I can go on alone. I've had a married life, children, why do I need a woman now? It really isn't about sex.* He had known even when he slept in a separate bedroom, it was about much more. He knew it was something magnificent filling his space, like rain and lavender clouds journeying across the sky. He reminded himself, *I did my best. I hope my daughters would come around someday.*

Martin sat in his Lazy Boy chair and watched the half-moon illuminating Lake Ontario. He sipped his cup of hot cocoa, and looking west, he saw the city houses and buildings stretched in glitters as candles in a church. He had been told one is never alone when a higher being resides in one's heart. His Penthouse seemed like a shrine, ideal for meditation and prayers.

His doorbell rang.

Martin opened the door—it was Azalia! He noticed she was dressed somewhat formal, in a pair of black dress pants and white blouse.

"Hello Martin, are you busy? May I come in?"

"Do come in Azalia. I was just relaxing."

"I am sorry I did not make it to the pool earlier. My mother hadn't been well, and I felt I should go see her."

"What's wrong with her?"

"Oh, just the flu. She's fine. I hadn't seen her for over two weeks. She is seventy-five and getting on."

“Would you like something to drink, tea or cocoa perhaps?”

“Herbal tea, if you have. I have to be up early for work.”

A Victorian tea set was on the living room table beside a stack of poetry books and tea biscuits in a fine bone-china plate.

“How was your banking today?” Azalia said.

"Well, I am glad for the closeness.”

“Closeness?” Azalia sounded puzzled.

“Oh, I don’t have to walk too far.”

“That’s good. I went to my church before visiting my mother, to light a candle for my father who passed away two years ago. He was a good man.”

Martin listened to Azalia’s remembrance of her father, the way her parents met, their forty-five years of marriage and the single red rose they kept on their bedroom dresser as a reminder of their love.

“That’s it! It’s all about friendship too isn’t Azalia? Your parents had become friends hadn’t they?”

“Yes, they understood each other and they talked and forgave each other when things went wrong. They harbored no grudges. My mother supported him when he got his education, became successful, when he lost his job; she cared for him when he became ill. My father never fooled around, you know.” Azalia sipped her tea.

Her smile is so gentle. "Do have some tea biscuits. Are you hungry? I can make good omelets."

"No thanks, I ate at my mother's."

"Come! Take a look at the night sky." Martin opened the drapery. Stars glittered in the cloudless sky.

"What a great view! You have a comfortable place here Martin."

"I am glad to make your friendship Azalia. Perhaps we can go out for dinner sometime?"

Azalia looked at Martin and smiled. "That would be lovely."

As Azalia approached the door to leave, Martin gave her a box of Godiva chocolate.

"Life can be like a box of chocolate."

"Perhaps. Goodnight," Azalia mumbled.

After Martin closed the door, through the window the half-moon appeared brighter. As he gazed at the painting on the wall of Jesus' mother, Mary, he noticed a glow he had not seen before. *Ah yes, soon a full moon!*

37. THINKING ALOUD
by Petamber PERSAUD

I nodded, murmuring to myself, "Some days are really different, Kumar-boy."

Like at dawn today my mom said I shouldn't talk to myself—only mad people do. But all I was doing then was muttering a prayer, beseeching *Bhagwan* to send the rains and save our farm from ruins.

I seldom pay my mom any heed because grown-ups were forever chastising children with proverbs and parables without offering any explanations, making disobedience all the more attractive. But today, *how* she said *what* she said about talking to *oneself* really bothered me, pestering me like a still, small voice.

In this state, I sneaked up on my *Aja,* relegated to live in a disused paddy hut. The old man was talking to himself, complaining how his immediate family does not care for him anymore, how society does not cater for the elderly, and how there was no proper retirement plan in place.

Slightly embarrassed, I retreated slowly as my paternal grandfather continued, "Look story—big fancy public servant tu'n not'ing now, heh!"

On my way to school I said hello to the gardener of the Krishna Temple.

She hushed me with an index finger to her cracked lips and continued muttering to a lovely yellow rose, calling it *the Maharani of India, the pride of Hindus.* The blooming of such a flower was a sign of rain, she said. She advised it to turn away from infidels before they *bad-eye* it, causing the rose to wither too quickly, thereby prolonging the dreaded drought.

When she was finished, she slipped off her *orhni* from her head before turning to me. "Wah yuh seh Kumar, boy?" A smile slowly lit up her face and the red *tika* in the middle of her forehead glowed brightly.

By now I was really worried, silently—as against not talking aloud to myself—trying to work out what's happening, why was everyone talking to himself or herself and why haven't I noticed it before!

I crept unto the back of a cart going my way to hear the milkman speaking to his donkey, Satan: "Babita nice-nice even though she doan pay on time but Rita wootliss, always poking fun at mih son, 'hiding between your father's legs again, like waan Inglish-duck'." The animal stopped at Babita's gap, without any prodding.

Not far off was the village beggar, a big and strapping man, budgeting and planning his next move, in a loud, clear voice: "If I can geh drunk on cheap rum, why waste money 'pon expensive liquor." With that he burst into an up-tempo song by Mohamed Rafi. And to crown it all, he brazenly reminded himself to get quality condoms—he was afraid of AIDS.

All this was too much for me—forthwith I started talking to myself, again. You see I couldn't retain every detail in my little head. So, talking to myself, listening to myself helped to put things in perspective. Talking to myself was natural, I now believed.

Which was what I was doing when I crawled home for dinner and caught my mom talking to herself: *How to make ends meet, how pa was drinking too much, and I always skulking from school and will never get a job.* She was talking to herself saying that *she was not getting help from my big sister whose interest was being drawn by the restless boys in the neighbourhood,* and *how to share the limited food—t'ree cassava-roti foh four people."*

I watched her, beating her bosoms, turning her face to heaven, asking God for help and spitting on the ground, telling the devil to go to hell. I watched my mom like she was going mad, behaving like Hari's mother who was sent to the madhouse for her violent gesticulating and for having continuous dialogue with a voice she alone could hear.

But I stayed silent, keeping a still tongue—another of my mother's many urgings—wondering why she didn't heed the advice she had given me earlier.

38. BEST BEFORE
by Ken PUDDICOMBE

The table had been set, the wine poured, the turkey carved, and Cutie was hoping they would have a peaceful dinner, for a change.

She had put up with Rommel's bickering and moaning for over twenty years, not only her, but their son Quince, the boy more so, in whom she saw growing signs of frustration. They were both tired of hearing the same lament, an unceasing barrage of complaints about life in Canada—the cold winters, hot summers, and everything in-between.

Rommel reached over for the platter with the turkey and paused before he filled his plate. "Of course," he said, "back in Guyana, we'd be having ham instead of turkey. Those were the days. Can you remember the Christmas in our first house, Cutie?"

She glanced at Quince who sighed, clearly exasperated hearing his father go on again about his boyhood days in the *colony with the highest standard of education in the Caribbean, when Georgetown was called the Garden City of the West Indies*.

Rommel had taken his position at the head of the table, as was customary on Christmas day. Cutie's place was at the opposite end, with faster access to the kitchen, Quince to the right of his father.

"Yes, Rommel, I remember," she said.

"Of course, that was long before you were born," Rommel said to Quince.

Rommel reached over for the wine decanter and filled his glass. "And we'd be having ginger-beer or sorrel drink instead of wine, garlic pork as a side dish, black cake for desert instead of apple pie. Yes sir, those were the days."

Quince sucked his teeth, but it was undetected during Rommel's noisy scooping of the turkey from the glass platter.

"Later on, Christmas day, we'd wander over to the neighbour and partake of their food and have a drink, perhaps more sorrel. As we grew older, we graduated to high-wine or rum." Rommel sighed. "Can't do that today. Too damn cold. Too much snow outside. Besides, how many people do you really know living on this street, anyhow? And even if you did know them, do you think you can hop over and have a drink with them? They would think you gone crazy.

"I know what you're going to say Quince. And I know you've heard it all before, but your childhood was a piece of cake compared to mine."

"Those days are long gone," Quince said. "They're not coming back, Dad. Can't you see that *Home* is here, now, in Canada."

"Home is where you born, boy. It's in the blood, in the DNA, yours and mine."

"You're forgetting Dad. You and mum were born there, I wasn't. So much for DNA, then."

"You still have a connection with the old country, boy, through me. It's a link that can never be broken."

"Well, I wish you'd stop talking about it. Why don't you *do* something about it?"

"But I will. It's the reason I built the house on the empty lot of land I bought when we were there. We should all go back, get away from this rat race."

Quince pushed his chair back and rose. "I can't speak for mum. But I'm never going back. It's too backward. Once was enough. You can go if you want, but don't plan on me joining you."

Quince headed for the foyer, picked his coat off the stand and went out to the driveway.

"Where's he going?" Rommel said. "It's Christmas day. Family time."

Cutie said, "He's going over to his girl to spend time with her."

"What's it now when a family can't have complete Christmas dinner and a relaxing evening together?"

"He's young. He's got a life of his own."

She pulled out an envelope from where it had been consigned under her place mat and turned it over to Rommel. "Merry Christmas."

He took the envelope, puzzled. "But we already open Christmas presents this morning."

"I know. It's just something else I got you."

The envelope was a half-size brown manilla, the flap tucked into the body.

He flipped it open and extracted a Christmas card. *To my husband. With best wishes for the years to come* printed on the front. Below the inscription, she'd written: "*Best Before January 31, 2000*". He opened the card, and something fell on the table.

Enclosed in blue wrapping paper was an airline

ticket. He smiled. "Oh, we going on vacation?" He took a closer look. "Ticket for Guyana. Sounds even better." Then his smile disappeared. "But it's only for me, Cutie!"

She nodded.

"Aren't you coming with me?"

She shook her head. "No Rommel. I'm giving you the chance to do what you've been dreaming of for so long."

"I don't understand. The house is built. It's why we've been sending money all these years, to go back and retire there."

There had been discussions and debates, all ending up in arguments when he raised the idea of building on the land he'd bought ten blocks from Lady's house on Independence Boulevard. It was *his* money, after all, that he sent to his sister for the project—a settlement for twenty-five years' service, after which he was laid off from Northern.

"It's *your* dream, Rommel. I might come to visit you sometime. I can't say right now. But I think you should go, even if it's to get it out of your system." She wanted to add: *I'm looking forward to not hearing you hassle me about it all the time*. But she didn't. It was Christmas.

"But I'm telling you, we can make it work. The house is completed—you've' seen the pictures that Lady sent. It's got all the conveniences we have here. It will be just like the old days, I tell you, even better."

Rommel pulled out a photograph from the inside pocket of his blazer and looked at it. He smiled. He'd started carrying that picture around with him since his sister sent it last year. The house looked splendid. A concrete structure, two floors, a verandah in front to catch the north-easterly sweeping in from the Atlantic, all surrounded by a high chain-link fence. Enough land at the rear for a vegetable garden. His sister had said it was the jewel of Independence Boulevard, the envy of the neighbourhood.

"I suppose you're right. Only time will tell. I'm hoping you will change your mind once I'm there, and join me," he said.

*

Rommel came out of the terminal pulling his suitcase, his old BWIA carry-on slung over his right shoulder.

At the end of a queue, he had to surrender his luggage ticket to two armed guards who compared the serial number with that on the suitcase and let him go. These were not the only armed guards he'd seen since arriving. They were spread throughout the terminal.

A tall man hailed him. "Heading for GT man? I can tekh you." The man attempted to grab his suitcase and he resisted. Someone grabbing his suitcase was not the right type of person to give his business.

The hand written sign—INDEPENDENCE BOULEVARD, written in black, bold letters, was up high at the rear of the crowd and he stopped short and doubled back to see who was holding it.

The man, about five feet three in height, was the shortest in the batch of taxi drivers crammed outside the arrivals area.

"You're going to Independence Boulevard?" Rommel said.

"Yes boss. I can tekh you there."

The man led the way out the terminal to the parking lot.

"And your name is?"

"Babooram, but you can call me Ram. Ah live right on Independence Boulevard, boss. I know it well."

"Before we go. How much is this going to cost me?"

"Not much boss. You got US or Canadian?"

"Canadian."

"How about if we settle for twenty-five? Tip included."

Ram placed the suitcase in the trunk of the old Morris Oxford and strapped the lid with rope. He opened the left door to the front and closed it behind Rommel, then took his place behind the wheel.

Rommel looked around the car, up and over, and to his right. Ram laughed. "Don' worry looking for seat belt, boss. The car got none. Besides, we in Guyana, you know. So you not breaking the law."

Ram turned the key in the ignition and the car sputtered to life. He took a careful look at his passenger before he pulled out of the parking lot. "You got a knowing face. Didn't you and your family live down by the Well Road off Independence Boulevard?"

"As a matter of fact, we did. That was way back in the fifties, before I left Guyana."

They left the airport behind and headed north on the single lane highway. A steady stream of traffic came in the opposite direction.

"Lots of traffic—are they all heading to the airport?"

Ram nodded. "Yes, but they early for the morning flight back to Toronto." Ram glanced in the rear view mirror. "How long you been away?"

"I left in nineteen sixty-four."

"And you never been back?"

"Once, briefly for a two-week vacation in 1980."

"Well, is a lot of changes in the country since then, some good, some bad."

"What's good?"

"Lots of money coming in from people like you coming back to take up residence. Building booming. Lots of people trading. The economy is growing fast, fast."

Rommel smiled. It was as he expected. "So, tell me about the bad, now."

Ram passed his left hand slowly across his scalp. He was practically bald, apart for a tuft of hair growing at the sides of his head.

"A lot of fraud. You still can't get something done without greasing somebody's palm in government. And crime increase, big, big time."

"I guess it's not much different from any developing country."

Ram shrugged. "Except, drug smuggling is a big t'ing, too." He laughed. "You just have to look at the big houses in Georgetown and ask yourself where the money coming from."

As they drove down the road, Rommel was amazed at the number of young people hanging around the bars, drinking and smoking. "What do the young people do for work?"

"They don' like working. They all want to go to America or Canada. Or they all waiting for some relative to send money back so they can live it up."

It was a cynical point of view that Rommel never heard expressed from the Guyanese expatriates in Canada. They all extolled the benefits of returning to live in Guyana, from the pleasant climate to the extent which their Canadian currency stretched.

"Where you going to live?" Ram said.

"I bought a piece of land and built my own house."

"That's nice. Coming back to live off the fat of the land or do business?"

"I'm retired now. Want to do nothing but relax and take it easy."

"And how about your family? They coming too?"

"Eventually."

"You 'ave relatives in Independence Boulevard?"

"My sister is Milady. They call her Lady. Her husband is Earnest but he died in nineteen-ninety-eight. Their son is Mitchell. They all live at 200. Do you know them?"

Ram glanced at him. "Everybody in the Boulevard know Mitchell. But Lady long gone. I think she living in one of the islands now. Might be Trinidad or Barbados,

I can't remember."

That was news to Rommel. It had been a couple of months since he'd been in touch with his sister, but she'd never told him of a plan to leave Guyana, certainly not in any of her letters to him. He'd been relying on her to smoothen his return and help him integrate back into the society he'd left so many years ago. And what was Ram implying when he said *everyone in the Boulevard knew Mitchell*?

"So, who is living in their old house at 200?"

"Is Mitchell living there. But is not an old house anymore, you know. He rebuild it. Is now the best looking house in the Boulevard."

Was there another reason why everyone knew Mitchell? His sister had told Rommel that her son had a reputation as someone who did everything in a big way. Smoked and drank excessively. Big time Gambler. Women all over the place. Mitchell was a security guard who worked sporadically. So, where did the money come from for him to enjoy his lifestyle? Was he also dealing drugs or involved in crime?

"Tell me what else you know about Mitchell?"

Ram squirmed in the driver's seat and shook his head. "Ah don' like to talk bad about people. What address you build the house?"

"Two-five-two."

Ram shook his head and lapsed into silence.

They came to the Boulevard. Ram made a right and Rommel was counting the house numbers as he passed. They came to an empty lot. Ram stopped the car and pointed in the direction of the lot. Even in the dark, Rommel was able to see, from the light cast by the two adjacent houses, that the property was overgrown with bramble bush and tall paragrass. But no house.

Rommel came out of the car, Ram behind him. They went closer to the lot. A dilapidated paling fence in front lay half-way to the ground. It looked as if it would collapse soon. The gate in the middle of the fence still hung on the top hinge.

"This can't be," Rommel said. "There must be some mistake."

Ram pointed to the house on the right. "That there is number two-fifty. Look at the sign." He pointed to the house on the left. "That there is two-fifty-four. This lot in the middle is two-fifty-two."

"Something's wrong. Lady sent me pictures of the house when it was being constructed and I have one of it completed." Rommel reached into his jacket pocket and pulled out the photograph. He turned it over to Ram who scrutinized it carefully.

"I know all the houses on the Boulevard. None look like that anywhere."

"There's got to be some mistake."

"Boss, is one of two things happen. Your sister Lady gone to the islands with the money. Or Mitchell rebuild the old house with it. Or both. Your guess is as good as mine."

"Take me to Mitchell. He must know what happened to all the money I sent back to his mother to build my house."

Ram took a few steps and paced back and forth. "Ah

don' think that's a good idea. That man deal in drugs and the underworld. People who deal with him disappear and never seen again."

"But what am I going to do? All my life savings were sunk into this property."

Ram sighed. He looked at his watch. "You still gat the land and be thankful you still gat your life. We can still make it for the return flight to Canada."

39. ODE TO JAI
By Cliff RAJKUMAR

The light of my life has abandoned me to the anguish of grief.

I lament this parting with wretched despair.
Your sweet fragrance and joyful infectious smile
Are forever etched in my heart.

Painful emotions overwhelm my intellect and rationality.
Foolishly, I question: *How can this be. Why you? Why me?*

Wisdom forsakes my better judgement
As I surrender to the agony of this priceless loss
Which haunts my mind and soul.

So suddenly and without warning,
The lord of death confined my precious gem
to the bosom of eternity.

Time has passed but the suffering lingers.
The bond of a father and son is unbreakable and undying.
The mystery of life and death is a secret
only the creator understands.

God knows best, I am told.
But the consolation is fleeting and hollow.

A lesson I have come to accept, with painful distress
and self-torture.

Visitors are we all, in this glorious miracle of life.
Yet! We cling and claim ownership to that which really belongs to time.
Now, I unwillingly surrender to the fate of destiny
Since...Impermanence does not discriminate.

Like the life-giving rain which comes to nurture mother earth,
In a timeless cycle of benevolence to create and sustain life.
So too, you came to give joy to all who were blessed to know you.

40. ON THE FRONTLINE
by Shabeena RAMJOHN

On the frontline,
Since March.

As a health worker I can tell you
this was the pivotal point of our paths.
This was just the beginning of a battle to be fought,
Our enemy we knew so little about,
Our patients still the priority, there was no doubt,
But like soldiers and captains with strategic plans,
With the Hippocratic oath in hand,
the doctors, nurses and technicians
fulfilled their jobs with compassion and dedication.

On the frontline,
Our lab-coats and protective gear don't make us invincible,
Our struggles are not always visible,
Behind PPE we are still human with families like yours,
So when you see us in scrubs on the roads at night,
We are just trying to get home and make sure our loved ones are alright,
When you see the nurse on her way to work,
Don't forget she has to prepare meals for her kids
and her shift was definitely not where her work began.

On the front line,
We may not have visible marks,
The hospitals and clinics are not amusement parks.
With our millions of voices,

We plead with you,
To stop transmission and curb the spread,
Listen to the words I have said,
Social distance is not a stretch,
But it keeps us from falling over the edge.
Wearing your mask and washing your hands,
It protects and saves a family,

From the front lines where we stand.

41. LIKE AMAZON RAIN I DANCE
by James RICHMOND

Drums!
Drums!
Drums!
Of One People.
Of One Nation.
Of One Destiny.
Drums of Guyana!
Amerindian drum!
African drum!
Indian drum!
Cumfa drum!
Masquerade drum!
The drums of Guyana!
When yuh hear the drums.

Like Amazon rain I dance
For the Amerindian drums tells the inspirational story
Of mystical legends and bequeathed legacy.
This is the history. *This* is the history.
I dance the dance of an old Amerindian.
I dance the dance of the Amerindians.

Like Amazon rain I dance
For the African drums becomes my soul
The tropical spirit I now behold!
Jubilant and enchanted, revisiting time and times of old
I dance the dance of an old African.
I dance the dance of the Africans.

Like Lightning in the rain I dance
For the Indian drums become my dream
And rise like a mystical streak, a vision unseen!
A vision of light, with *ghungrus* and sari
I dance the dance of an old Indian.
I dance the dance of the Indians.

Like clouds of fire I dance
For the Cumfa drums speak to me.
Spiritual flames across the floor; resurrected and free!
I dance the dance of Cumfa.
I dance the dance of Cumfa.

Like Amazon rain,
Lightning and clouds of fire I dance,
For the masquerade drums awake my soul.
Unity is here foretold! Unity is a laudable goal.
My tropical spirit, like flickering lights unfold!
Now dance the dance of Guyana.
Now dance the dance of Guyana.

Like Amazon rain,
Lightning and clouds of fire I dance,
For the masquerade drums awake my soul.
Unity is here foretold! Unity is a laudable goal.
Chinese, Portuguese and Mixed Races untold
My tropical spirit, like flickering lights unfold!
Now dance the dance of Guyana.
Now dance the dance of Guyana.

When yuh hear the drums!

42. I CAN'T BREATHE
by Ray WILLIAMS

"I can't breathe," cried George Floyd
His head twisting and turning
His voice weak and muffled
Not attached to a Covid-19 respirator
Nor caused by an asthma attack
But more deliberately under the oppressive knee
Of a white Minneapolis Policeman
Who ground George's bloodied face
Further into the unyielding asphalt roadway
Ignoring the cries of horrified bystanders
While fellow Police Officers stood by
Watching dispassionately as George's life ebbed away

George was not the first, nor will he be the last
Since centuries before countless numbers
Of his former African ancestors
Likewise, couldn't breathe, suffering the stench
Of the all-dehumanizing slave trade
Sick, starving and dying in droves
Their carcases soon thrown to the sharks
As they, for months crossed the 'Middle Passage'
Bound for the promised lands of the Americas

The survivors among them couldn't breathe as well
Hanging by the noose swaying in the branches
Of the plantation's giant Weeping Willow trees
Mocked by hateful mobs in hooded white robes
Including women and giggling children
Viewing them only as freak-show entertainment

Pity George's oppressed forefathers and mothers
Toiling endless days under the blistering sun
Picking bales upon bales of lung-stifling cotton
Closely watched by their horse-riding white overseers
Whips in hand, ready to raise yet more bloody welts
Upon their bent and work-weary backs should they
Dare be sick, unwilling or God forbid, rebellious

Like George, the courageous Civil Rights marchers
Of the Nineteen Fifties and Sixties couldn't breathe either
Charged upon and pummelled by truncheon-wielding Policemen
Bowled over and near drowned under crowd-clearing fire hoses
Their powerful jets aimed and spewed upon them as authorized
By the brutal Jim Crow laws of the Southern States

"Black Lives Matter," cries today's generation of protesters
Where black, white, brown and all those in-between march
Hand-in-hand against continued racism and inequality
And despite dreaded slavery and segregation now long abolished
Its dark clouds of hatred and racism still hover in all quarters

The fight will carry on to that glorious day when
The sunshine of love and fellowship lights the way
Not only for our children's children, but for future

George Floyd's of this world, who will no longer be restrained
But rightly breathe the fresh air of freedom and equality
Long promised to us all.

ABOUT THE AUTHORS

HABEEB ALLI

Habeeb Alli has a Masters in Islamic Theology and Arabic Language from Deoband Islamic University in India and a Diploma in Journalism from Delhi. The author of twenty-six publications on Canadian Muslims, Interfaith and Poetry including the recent *Wild Lavender*, is also a member of the Canadian Council of Imams. Habeeb holds several directorships including the Interfaith Committee called *Abraham Festival in Peterborough* and the *One Love Family Services*. Imam Alli was recognized by the Junctian Network and Vigor Humanitarian Award in 2020. In addition to being Federal Chaplain with Correctional Services Canada and Spiritual care Coordinator at Cummers Lodge, and sitting on a number of community boards, Habeeb is the President of Pakaraima Writers Assocation. Habeeb blogs at https://whispersofkaieteur.blogspot.com/

JEROME BRANCHE

Jerome Branche teaches at the University of Pittsburgh. His books and research cover Africana Literature in the Hispanic World, Postcolonial Studies, and Critical Race Theory. He hails from Agricola/Rome, Greater Georgetown, Guyana.

ALICIA DANIELS

Alicia Latoya Daniels, born in Georgetown, Guyana, is a poet, teacher, author and a founder of A & J Creative Designs Plus. Trained as an Educator, she has been involved in Primary level education for over a decade. She discovered her talent for writing poetry in her teens, a gift encouraged by presentations in her local church on occasions such as Mother's Day, Father's Day, New Year's Eve, and Easter. She was an adult category finalist in a "Trafficking In Persons Poetry Competition". Her book, "A Poet's Mind- A Collection of Inspiring Poems", was compiled to provide encouragement and raise awareness of some of the challenges that continue to present themselves in society. She can be contacted by email: aliciadaniels592@gmail.com.

FRANCIS QUAMINA FARRIER

Francis Quamina Farrier won the First Prize in a National Schools Essay-Writing competition while he was in Primary School. He also won First Prize in the National Playwriting Competition when Guyana became Independent in 1966. He further gained national prominence as the writer of the Caribbean's first ever locally produced Radio soap opera; *The Tides of Susanburg* which was so popular that a sequel - *The Girl From Susanburg* - was produced. Many of Farrier's short plays were also produced and aired on Radio, over the years.

LISA FREEMANTLE

Lisa Freemantle lives in Newmarket Ontario and has taught in Catholic Schools in the Greater Toronto area for nearly 30 years. She the author of a number of books published by Novalis and has also produced a number of CD's. She has been writing poetry since she was a child. Lisa is also related to poet Martin Carter who was her father's cousin. She is married with three grown children.

PETER JAILALL

Peter Jailall (BA, BEd, MA, OISE/U of T) is a teacher, poet and storyteller. He began his teaching career in September 1965 at Enmore Government School in Guyana after graduating from the Government Training College for Teachers. He continued his teaching career in Canada between 1970 to 1998. He has published five books of poetry. Peter volunteers with CUSO as a teacher-trainee in Guyana. He received the 2010 Guyana Cultural Association Award for his work in Rural Education in Guyana and in 2011 received the Marty's Award for Established Literary Arts in Mississauga, Ontario. Since his retirement, Peter has conducted workshops on Poetry Writing, in schools across Guyana and Canada. He lives in Mississauga where he gardens in summer.

IAN McDONALD

Born in Trinidad, Ian was educated at Queens Royal College and Cambridge University. His career has spanned several decades in Business, Sports and Literature. He is the recipient of Guyana's Golden Arrow of Achievement and has won the Guyana Prize for Literature – Poetry three times. The University of the West Indies in 1997 awarded him honorary Doctorate Of Letters. He has been a Fellow of The Royal Society Of Literature since 1970 and has edited and co-edited numerous collections and anthologies. His novel *The Hummingbird Tree* (1969) was made into a BBC film. He has published seven poetry collections in addition to short stories and two collections of essays and speeches. He continues to write on cricket and poetry.

JANET NAIDU

Janet Naidu is a poet, writer and educator with expertise in workplace equity, diversity and inclusion. She has three collections of poetry. *Winged Heart* (Greenheart, 1999) was short-listed for the Guyana Prize for Literature, Poetry category, in 2000. Her other collections include *Rainwater* (Greenheart, 2005), and *Sacred Silence* (Hansib, 2009). Her poetry includes themes of migration, exile, settlement, identity, struggle, feminism, survival and more. Some of her poems have also been published in the University of the West Indies Journal for Women Studies, and Anthologies such as *A Bouquet of Flowers* and *Sudden Thunder*, Canada. Naidu is the founder of PAKARAIMA Writers' Association. Naidu has a BA in Political Science and Caribbean Studies and an LL.B (Bachelor of Law).

PETAMBER PERSAUD

Enabler of Guyanese Literature, television producer, literary activist and events coordinator, Petamber is the author of *An Introduction to Guyanese Literature* and *The Balgobin Saga* among other books.

KEN PUDDICOMBE

Professional [CPA.CMA] Accountant Ken Puddicombe provided controllership for a number of companies before he retired to pursue his first love of writing which has appeared in newspapers and literary journals. Originally from British Guiana [now Guyana], he immigrated to Canada and still lives there. *Racing With The Rain*, his first novel is set in British Guiana, Cuba, Canada and Guyana. His second novel *Junta*, published in 2014 in the fictional island of Saint Anglia. His collection of short stories *Down Independence Boulevard* was released in 2017. His first book of poems *Unfathomable and Other Poems* was released in 2020. His genre is fiction, especially focused on Canada, the Caribbean and Guyana. His website: www.kenpud.wordpress.com

CLIFF RAJKUMAR

Cliff Rajkumar is a former senior management executive

with ITT, GE and Deutsche Bank. After a very successful and fulfilling career, widely travelled for his international assignments, projects and responsibilities as a senior executive for those Global organizations for over thirty years, he took early retirement and focused on social and community services and involvement. Cliff has a passion and keen interest in the evolution and history of civilization and the common genetic and ancestral linkage of all people. He is a fervent advocate for environmental protection. As well, he embraces unity in diversity and the peaceful coexistence of all races. He has written many articles and essays on Hinduism—a subject of deep interest and passion for him.

SHABEENA RAMJOHN

Shabeena Ramjohn is a Dental Surgeon. This journey all began when she was awarded a place at The Bishops' High School. Her career choice was deeply influenced by the kind, caring nature of her parents and the love of her brother. It is through their support that she was able to complete her bachelor's degree in Dental Surgery at the University of Guyana. One would wonder how a Dentist gets involved in poetry, but she knew to be a well-rounded individual, she needed to play just as hard as she worked. Poetry now is an integral hobby that helps her to be appreciative, grounded and to continue learning in all avenues of life. She can be reached at: sr1994316@yahoo.com

---

JAMES C. RICHMOND

James C. Richmond is a poet, preacher and author of the books *Reflections of Today*, *Where the Pomeroon Meets* and *On the Window of My Skin*. He served as a member of the Mayor of New York Clergy Advisory Council under Bill de Blasio and as a community advocate/organizer on the Faith Advisory Taskforce during the covid-19 pandemic. Richmond has used his talent in writing poetry on the *Book of Daniel*, and the *Book of Revelation*—his books are entitled, *The Language of Daniel* (2021) and *The Language of Revelation* (due 2022) including a chronicle of the pandemic. James has been a consummate performer of his poetry over 30 years and is continuing his studies in Theology at Andrews University.

RAY WILLIAMS

Ray Williams is an author, photographer, woodcarver, and traveler whose work has been published in Trip Advisor under the pen name *817 Ray*. He is a member of Writers Community of Durham Region, winning First Prize in their competition for his story *The Last Leaf of Autumn*. He is currently an active member of Pakaraima Writers Association. Over his writing career he has produced over 40 short stories and 28 poems, and his travels have included many parts of Asia, Europe, Africa and South America. He retired after a long and distinguished career in the Ontario Public Service, also serving in numerous committees for law enforcement, immigration and Correctional Services. He can be reached at: raywilliams4243@gmail.com

MORE BOOKS FROM MIDDLEROAD PUBLISHERS

www.middleroadpublishers.ca

ALL AVAILABLE ON AMAZON

In Paperback, Hard Cover and eBook

MiddleRoad | Publishers

"Making literature see the light of day."

A TIME TO LOVE AN A TIME TO DIE

By Michael Joll

Finely drawn characters. Visually dramatic, tense and emotionally satisfying, this is one of the finest novels of the Great War. In this poignant story, the writing stands in stark contrast with the unvarnished brutality of trench warfare.

ATTITUDE

By Dave Moores

Fresh, gritty and laced with dry humour, Attitude is a fast-paced story readers of all ages won't want to put down. It's dead of winter and an outbreak of weird stuff, random acts of vandalism are unsettling the citizens of Southmead.

DOWN INDEPENDENCE BOULEVARD AND OTHER STORIES

by Ken Puddicombe

"A brilliant collection of stories telling the tales of people forced to leave their homes...craving the past, escaping from racial conflicts and dictatorship..."—Judith Kopacsi Gelberger, author of *Heroes Don't Cry*.

GABRIELLE

By Michael Joll

Gabrielle transcends time and space, taking the reader on a journey to Poland, France, Holland

and Israel as she searches for her identity.

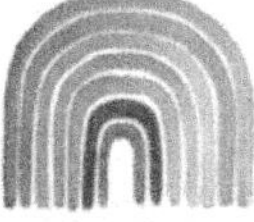

I WENT TO THE END OF THE RAINBOW

by Pramita Chakraborty

A beautifully illustrated, captivating tale about a young child who can't sleep and embarks on a adventure through the colours of the rainbow.

JUNTA

By Ken Puddicombe

"A gripping story (of) an imperfect democracy...the tension...builds increasingly from page to page."—Rico Downer, author of *There Once Was a Little England*

LOVE HAS TWO MOONS

By Franklin Mohan

With humour, insight and sensitivity, Franklin Mohan peels back the subtle layers of prejudice and racism in North American and Caribbean society—Raymond Holmes, author of *Witnesses and other short stories*

MEET ME AT THE FOUR CORNERS

Anthology

Twenty-six stories, fiction and non-Fiction, some of them prize winning submissions from the writers of the Brampton Writers' Guild, are featured in this collection.

PEOPLE OF GUYANA

By Ian McDonald and Peter Jailall

"These beautifully crafted poems are shaped by their generosity of spirit and abundant capacity for empathy and fun..." —Clem Seecharan

PERSONS OF INTEREST

By Michael Joll

"Exotic and intriguing! Joll brilliantly captures the reader's interest with vivid imagery and a relentless sleuth." —Phyllis Humby, short story writer, poet and novelist.

PERFECT EXECUTION AND OTHER STORIES

by Michael Joll.

"Michael Joll is a master of surprise endings, but they never seem forced. He always stays true to his characters and their worlds." —Nancy Kay Clark, author and editor, *CommuterLit.com*

POEMS FOR MARY

By Ian Mc Donald

"The garden which my wife has created, it is as much a work of art as a painting by a master spirit or a piece of perfect music by a composer."—Ian Mc Donald

RACING WITH THE RAIN

By Ken Puddicombe

"Puddicombe's brilliant novel…an historic political conflict in Guyana, during the Cold War and the cold cynicism and tragic irony of a state sacrificed to super-power hegemony." -Frank Birbalsingh, author of *Novels and The Nation: Essays in Canadian*

RUTHLESS RHYTHMS

By Judith Gelberger

Gelberger takes the reader into the world of terror and oppression…while surrounding him with warm love and tenderness.

THE GARDEN

By Ian McDonald

Ian McDonald's poems are full of light and love. His easy style about the beauty of nature connects with his readers far and wide.

UNFATHOMABLE AND OTHER POEMS

by Ken Puddicombe

These poems cover a variety of themes, all connected to a childhood growing up in British Guiana, the rise of nationalism and the pre- and post-independence eras.

WEALTH THROUGH REAL

ESTATE INVESTING

By Jay Brijpaul

Jay Brijpaul has tapped his vast experience and expertise in the Real Estate industry. This book provides comprehensive coverage of What, How, When, Where to invest in real estate.

WINDWARD LEGS

By Dave Moores

A pungent cocktail of choppy romance, corporate larceny and the thrills and spills of sailboat racing, Windward Legs is the rousing and captivating story of a woman's journey to rediscover who she is.

WITNESSES AND OTHER STORIES

By Raymond Holmes

"Suspenseful, historical, futuristic and riveting…stories and characters who will stay with you." —Bruce A. Hanson, Award winning author of adult and children's fiction.

Made in United States
Orlando, FL
07 June 2022

18595931R00075